柔波里
的
水草

李美华 著

The
Waterplants
in the Waves

外语教学与研究出版社
FOREIGN LANGUAGE TEACHING AND RESEARCH PRESS
北京 BEIJING

图书在版编目（CIP）数据

柔波里的水草：汉英对照 / 李美华著. —— 北京 ：外语教学与研究出版社，2019.3（2019.8 重印）
ISBN 978-7-5213-0808-2

Ⅰ. ①柔… Ⅱ. ①李… Ⅲ. ①诗集－中国－当代－汉、英 Ⅳ. ①I227

中国版本图书馆 CIP 数据核字 (2019) 第 045329 号

出 版 人 徐建忠
责任编辑 巢小倩
责任校对 孔乃卓
封面设计 郭 莹
出版发行 外语教学与研究出版社
社 址 北京市西三环北路 19 号（100089）
网 址 http://www.fltrp.com
印 刷 北京九州迅驰传媒文化有限公司
开 本 650×980 1/16
印 张 13
版 次 2019 年 3 月第 1 版 2019 年 8 月第 2 次印刷
书 号 ISBN 978-7-5213-0808-2
定 价 39.90 元

购书咨询：（010）88819926 电子邮箱：club@fltrp.com
外研书店：https://waiyants.tmall.com
凡印刷、装订质量问题，请联系我社印制部
联系电话：（010）61207896 电子邮箱：zhijian@fltrp.com
凡侵权、盗版书籍线索，请联系我社法律事务部
举报电话：（010）88817519 电子邮箱：banquan@fltrp.com
物料号：308080001

记载人类文明
沟通世界文化
www.fltrp.com

诗意剑桥（代序）

这辈子最幸运的，莫过于有机会到美国哈佛大学和英国剑桥大学访学，而这两所大学所在的地方，恰巧都叫剑桥。美国的剑桥在波士顿，英国的剑桥则是独立的一个市。在美国的剑桥，我从一个读者变成一个作者。而在英国的剑桥，我继续我的诗歌之旅，用诗歌记录了我顺与不顺掺杂的访学经历和忧思遐想。

2000 年，我有幸获得哈佛燕京学社的赞助，到哈佛大学进行了为期一年半的访学。这次访学，收获颇丰。学业上，我完成了博士论文的写作，回国以后顺利通过答辩，从博士生变成了博士。事业上，获得更多学养的我回国后从副教授变成教授。而除了学业和事业上的收获外，我也从一个读者变成了一个作者。我在哈佛大学开始了第一首诗歌的创作，发表了第一首英文诗歌，散文写作也是从这里开始的。这以后，写作渐渐成了我的生活方式。从哈佛大学回来以后，我出版了第一部中英对照诗集——《忆泠短诗选》，后来又陆续出版了三部诗集——《忆泠世纪诗选》《忆泠自选集——水声泠泠》和《雪落无痕》，而散文集《抒情的岁月——哈佛访学散记》更是对哈佛访学生活的一种记忆。

2016 年，作为福建省百千万人才工程省级人选，我又获赞助前往英国访学半年。在选择学校的时候，我在剑桥大学和牛津大学之间反复斟酌，最终还是选择了剑桥大学。其原因不言自明，吸引我到剑桥大学的正是著名诗人徐志摩。作为剑桥的特殊学生，徐志摩曾经在剑桥大学呆过一年，留下了脍炙人口的佳作——《再别康桥》。我想循着诗人的步履，走读他呆过的剑桥，寻觅他遗落的诗情。

剑桥是个小城，小巧而典雅，漂亮而浪漫。剑桥之所以能闻名于世，当然是因为一流学府剑桥大学。国王学院、女王学院、三一学院和圣约翰学院等为剑桥留下了高贵而古朴的建筑，也为剑桥留下了遗世独立的气质。穿城而过的剑河，也就是徐志摩诗里的康河，经过剑桥大学的七个学院，给剑桥带来特有的风情。剑河两岸，莺飞草长，金柳依依。我经常沿着剑河漫步，看天鹅闲游，观野鸭戏水，看学生划船，望白云悠悠。剑河的柔波，河里的水草，天空的白云，天边的晚霞，挂在树梢的月亮，还有常绿的草地，食草的牛群，香气袭人的大树，横亘剑河的桥梁，无不让我顿生灵感，诗情激荡。

也是命数使然，短短的六个月访学生活，我却遭遇了脚被撞伤乃至半个多月无法出门的惨境。之后又生疾病，经历一番焦虑与挣扎，不得已回国医治。短短半年，从联系学校的顺利到只身奔赴英伦的孤寂，从对剑桥美景的迷醉到生病回国的折腾，经历可谓丰富，心路可谓复杂。幸福与痛苦同在，顺境与逆境并存。所有这一切，都成了我诗歌创作的灵感来源，一首首诗歌便像一股股灵泉，从心底汩汩流出。

在剑桥访学期间，我总共写了76首诗歌，主题不一而足，有对剑桥美景的抒写，有在剑河边漫步闲坐时的遐想，有脚受伤而被禁足期间的郁闷和纾解，有疾病未确诊时的焦虑与不安，有对痛苦和病情的无奈与接受，还有对生命本身的思考与感叹，自然也有离别时的不舍与伤感。这些诗歌，是我对剑桥大学访学生活的点滴描述，也是对我生命中一个特殊阶段的特殊纪念。以中英对照的形式出版，是我对这一阶段生活最为合适的记忆方式。诗集题目《柔波里的水草》直接从徐志摩的诗句里撷取，而做一棵剑河柔波里的水草同样也是我的梦想。回国以后，经常想起剑桥，想起那段时间的经历，特出此诗集，以作纪念。是以代序！

2017 年 9 月 8 日于厦门寓所

作者简介

　　李美华，笔名忆泠，福建连城人。厦门大学外文学院教授，美国哈佛大学、伊利诺大学和英国剑桥大学访问学者。中国散文学会会员，福建省作家协会会员。主要作品有专著《英国生态文学》《琼·狄第恩作品中新新闻主义、女权主义和后现代主义的多角度展现》，译著《飘》（译林版）、《德黑兰的屋顶》《动物农庄》（上海文艺版），诗集《忆泠自选集——水声泠泠》《雪落无痕》，散文集《抒情的岁月——哈佛访学散记》《邂逅流年》及小说《永远没多远》等。

目 录

1. 雨中国王

寒冬的料峭
催发春天的羞赧
花儿含蓄地开放
鸟儿羞涩地鸣叫

缠绵的小雨
恋上了碧绿的青草
用湿润的温柔
给青草柔情的拥抱

国王昂首挺胸
继续展示一如既往的骄傲
曲径
岂止是通幽
雨水洗过的青石板
透出别样的妖娆

季节虽然未到
春天的情愫
已经在蓄积力量
等待春姑娘无理的骚扰

心底
冬眠的情感被唤醒
萦绕于心
而熟悉的那个影像
在剑桥的雨里
茫茫渺渺

2016-03-10, 07:34

1. *The King in the Rain*

The coldness in late winter
Hastens the signs of early spring
Flowers are about to blossom
While the birds are agreeably singing

The rain sprinkles in the air
With love to the greenery
It embraces the grass
With its tenderness of humidity

Standing majestically in Cambridge
King's College continuously
Displays its pride and authority
Moisturized by the drizzle
The winding granite path
Is both enchanting and fascinating

Though still in winter
Spring is coming near
It will again reign over the earth
With its overwhelming power

Love wakes up from hibernation
And the familiar image
Appears in the rain of Cambridge
Indistinct and obscure

03/10/2016

2. 河畔的金柳

择水边而居
你是水边的仙子
当晨曦微露
你伸开慵懒的腰肢
睁开惺忪的眼睛

以水为镜
你用心打扮自己
金色的丝绦缕缕
如瀑布垂挂水面
少女浣发的倩影
装点了严寒的冬季

纵使寒意侵袭
你的金色
逆转了灰色的主旋律
于是
冬日里
你的美丽
溢出阵阵醉人的暖意

河畔的金柳
岂能是谁的新娘
你的美丽
是自然的恩赐
想娶你
无疑是夸父逐日
不自量力

2. The Golden Willow at the River Cam

Living by the waterside
You are undoubtedly a fairy
When the day breaks
You stretch yourself indolently
And open your still sleepy eyes

You dress up and make up
With water as the mirror
The twigs droop over water
Just like a maiden's blond hair
Though it is still chilly in winter
Your gentle warmth dispels its coldness

Winter is generally grey and gloomy
But your golden skin has changed the theme
Chilliness in the sky
Is balanced by the warmth
Sipping out from your beauty

The golden willow at the River Cam
Is not the bride of a certain man
She is a gift by nature
No one deserves such a bounty
With his mortal ability

不由自主地爱上你
但我不求你的回应
请你尽情展示你的美丽
而我
只要能经常看见你
于爱
俨然足矣

2016-03-13，10:08

I cannot help falling in love with you
But I don't need your feedback
I will be just as happy as ever
If I can see you every day
And enjoy your infinite beauty

03/13/2016

3. 宿命

有些事
注定要发生
不想宿命
却逃不过
冥冥之中的定数

心里掠过的
只是一种预感
却准得出奇
可对此
却无能为力

发生便发生了
也无须怨怼不已
谨记
不管这世界发生过什么
明天
太阳照样会升起

2016-03-18，01:08

3. Foreordination

Certain things are doomed to take place
You just cannot avoid them
As they are foreordinations

A premonition in mind
Has become as true as the sky
I can only accept it
Though I'd rather not encounter it

No need to complain
At any misfortune
Just remember
No matter what happens
Tomorrow
The sun also rises

03/18/2016

4.康桥有感

有人轻轻地走了
又有人轻轻地来
一百年悄然逝去
剑桥的西天边上
一如既往地
飘着绚丽的云彩

没带走一片云彩
却留下了满腹诗怀
康河畔的诗句
陪伴长篙撑过的小船
随水草在水中摇摆

石桥依旧
在康桥的柔波里荡漾
金柳垂泪
兀自抒发昔人已逝的悲哀

芸芸众生
谁又能遗世千古
皆是过客
哪怕是旷世奇才

作别的
岂止是西天的云彩
还有浮云般飘过的
钻心的痛
恒久的伤
逝去的爱

2016-03-18，07:50

10

4. *Thoughts on the River Cam*

Very quietly someone takes his leave
Just as someone else quietly comes
One hundred years has passed
In the western sky of Cambridge
The rosy clouds are still lingering high

Without taking away a cloud
Xu Zhimo left a poetic heart behind
The poem on the stone beside the River Cam
Is dancing with the waterplants gracefully
While the boats are poled upstream and downstream

The stone bridge over the river
Reflects itself in the waves as usual
While the golden willows are lamenting
On the great poet's passing

The world is filled with people
But no living beings can be immortal
All are just passing travellers
Including the geniuses in all ages

Goodbye
The rosy clouds in the western sky
Goodbye
The unbearable pains
Permanent sadness
And already lost love

03/18/2016

5. 灵犀

栖息在细枝上
你静静地梳洗
沐浴着晨光
展现一种特有的孤寂

这棵尚未苏醒的树
难道是你的领地
抑或是你知悉我的到来
特意以你的方式
表示对我的欢迎

看到你的第一眼起
我便意会到一种灵犀
在异国的第一天
不期然与你相遇
就算不是至亲
也已经是近邻

我默默地
看着你晨妆的背影
看出了一种独立
看出了一种激情
看出了一种不屈

接下来的日子里
请你经常造访我的窗棂
你我可以惺惺相惜
同享英伦特有的孤寂

2016-03-18, 20:18

5. Understanding

Perching on the twig
You are washing and dressing
In the light of the early morning
Typical solitude is clearly seen

The tree that is still sleeping
Serves as your territory
Is it that you've known my arrival
So that you use this peculiar way
To welcome me

At the first sight of you
A kind of understanding
Has dawned on me
Meeting you on the first day
In a faraway country
We are neighbors though not relatives

Watching you quietly in the morning sunlight
I've sensed independence
Passion and unyieldingness

In days to come
Welcome you to perch on my window
So that we can appreciate each other
And enjoy solitude in England together

03/18/2016

6. 生命的断点

或许
那就是一劫
不是以这种方式
就会以别的方式度过
这一劫
成了生命中一个断点

那一刻
记忆全然空缺
来不及想
也没能力想
意识恢复之际
袭来无奈的虚怯

断点重新接上
痛感渐渐袭来
生命
脆弱如斯
总会被外力所熔断
断点与终点之间
只是瞬间的转换
未及思考
无法选择
一切的一切
就将烟消云散

有过生命的断点
争强成了天真
好胜未免痴傻
只有豁达
才是点亮生命的
唯一光亮

2016-03-19, 09:28

6. *The Breaking Point of Life*

Maybe
That is a disaster
One way or another
Serving as a breaking point in life

At that very moment
Everything is in a void
There is no time for me to think
Or to say
Thinking is beyond my ability
When consciousness comes back
Overwhelming weakness comes over me

Severe pain attacks me
As life enters absolute fragility
Between birth and death
There are many breaking points
When one of them comes over
Death is so near
No time to think reasonably
And no choice is available
To change the inevitability

Having experienced the breaking point in life
I have abandoned the desire to excel
Knowing that the most important thing in life
Is to be optimistic and open-minded

03/19/2016

7. 寂静

静得出奇
没有一丝声响
只听见自己
心跳的声音

剑桥的风
在无形的空气中穿行
想听风吟
却只有树枝
微微点头致意

剑河的水
平静如镜
打破宁静的
只有划过的小船
和天鹅野鸭荡起的涟漪

当阳光叩响窗棂
把我从睡梦中唤醒
我拉开窗帘
迎进晨曦

简单生活
高尚思考
每天例行的程序
吻合了华兹华斯的诗句

孤寂中生活
宁静中思考
致远处
是远山的岑净
和雪落无痕的心迹

2016-03-22, 08:07

7. Silence

With no sound around me
Silence dominates everything
What I can hear
Is only my heart's beating

The wind in Cambridge
Is blowing in the air, unseen
I want to hear the wind's singing
Only to find the branches nodding

The surface of the water in the River Cam
Is as quiet as a mirror
When the boats are poling through
Water ripples with swans and wild ducks
Swimming and dating as always

When the sunlight kisses the windowpane
I wake up from my dream
I pull open the curtain
To welcome the early morning

Simplify, simplify
To ponder seriously over life
What I do every day
Is in harmony with Wordsworth's poetry

To live in solitude
And to think in silence
Living a quiet life
Will lead you to the purity of snow
And serenity of holy mountains

03/22/2016

8. 迎春花

等了好些日子
墙角的迎春花
终于迎旭日开放

艳丽嫩黄
耀眼灿烂
压制了所有
迫不及待冒头的绿芽
舍我其谁的霸气
无法阻挡

墙角的迎春花
孤寂中适时的陪伴
天气虽还寒冷
心里已撒满一片春光

2016-03-22，11:06

8. *Winter Jasmines*

To meet with my expectation
The winter jasmines at the corner of the wall
Finally blossom in the sunshine

The yellow tenderness of the flowers
Dwarf the eager green leaves
Its arrogance is so overwhelming
That it can defeat anything

Sweet winter jasmines
Serve as solitary companions to me
Though the weather is still chilly
My heart is greeting a warm spring

03/22/2016

9. 窗外的风景

早春三月
天气微寒
窗外的风景
已是一片春光

一棵垂柳
尚未冒出绿芽
纤弱的枝条
却在微风中摇荡

这点动感
吸引了巢中的小鸟
纷纷在枝头栖息
从窗口窥探
窗内禁足人的忧伤

墙角的迎春花
终于不顾一切地开放
装点了窗外的风景
也慰藉了人的愁肠

2016-03-22，11:24

9. Window View

March is still chilly
While quietly comes the early spring
The window view
Has displayed the season evidently

The branches of a weeping willow
Are swaying with the breeze
When green leaves are nowhere to see

The birds in the nest are seduced
To perch on the twigs
They peer at the lady inside
Who is deprived of freedom unfortunately

The winter jasmines at the corner
Finally blossom splendidly
They merge into the view outside the window
Comforting the unlucky lady generously

03/22/2016

10. 梦 · 现实

梦里
一切都很忙乱
行装准备好了
却又被彻底遗忘
来到海滩
却发现未着泳装
成为别人的笑谈

现实中
异常成了正常
郁闷中
与迟到的春意对话
读出各自心怀的忧伤

顺境逆境
总在不停地转换
虽说物极必反
又何尝不是否极泰来
抑或是塞翁失马

禁足的忧伤
演绎成思维的潇洒
码字越发轻狂
美煞窗外霸气的迎春花

2016-03-24, 9:22

10. *Dream Versus Reality*

In the dream
Everything is messy
Packing is ready
But is forgotten completely
I arrive at the seashore
Only to find myself not in a swimming suit
I then become the laughing stock of all

In reality
Everything is orderly
I melancholily start a dialogue
With the late spring
And we understand each other's agony

Favorable circumstances or adversity
They are always changing
A thing turns to its opposite if pushed too far
But after a storm always comes calm
And a loss can turn out to be a gain

The sorrow brought about by restriction
Leads to fantastic imagination
Writing becomes so easy
Which is envied and admired
Even by the arrogant winter jasmines

03/24/2016

11. 孤独

流云从空中飘过
忧伤在心里存留
孤独
是一杯寂寞的酒
越饮越浓稠

世界
是一个孤独的空壳
天体
万物
生灵
挤占着所有的空间
摩肩接踵
却互不搭理

我知道
你在空间的那一头
我在空间的这一头
两不相望
却各自啜饮孤独
不再交流

春天虽已到来
冬意尚未褪尽
横亘半空的彩虹
不再绚丽多彩
瀑布飞溅而下
水雾弥漫开来
笼罩了世界的孤独

孤独
依旧
向世人展示胜利者的笑容

2016-03-26，17:13

11. Solitude

The clouds are drifting in the sky
Melancholy dwells in the mind
Solitude is like wine
The more you drink
The more loneliness you will find

The universe is a void of solitude
Stars, objects and living things
Jostle together
Yet ignore each other

I know
You are at the far end of the ocean
And I am right here at the seaside
We cannot see each other
But enjoy solitude respectively
Instead of communicating

Spring has come
Though it is still cold
The rainbow in the sky seems not colorful
The waterfall gushes down with mist
Covering the solitude of the universe

Solitude
Just as ever
Displays its smile of a winner

03/26/2016

12. 另一个剑桥的回忆

时间悄然逝去
一切皆成往昔
哈佛的记忆
萦绕在脑际
成了此生靓丽的风景

而立之年已过
对世事犹自不明
剑桥的风雨
见证了一段成熟的心迹

哈佛校园里的漫步
牵出尘封的诗意
满腹忧伤的思绪
在剑桥的风雨中穿行

怀德纳图书馆里
与书中的人物同悲同喜
课堂讲座的学人
慰藉我求知的心灵

桑树上小鸟的吟唱
带来内心的欢欣
查尔斯河畔的雁鸣
吻合心底的悲情

12. *In Memory of Another Cambridge*

Time is flying
And everything is passing
The memory of Harvard lingers in the mind
Which has become a splendid view in life

While in the thirties
I still felt confused about many things
The experience at Harvard University
Witnessed a period of maturity

Taking walks at Harvard yard
Led to long-forgotten poetic flavor
Lots of melancholy thinking
Was flying in the rain and wind
Of lovely and sublime Cambridge

In Widener Library
I kept company with heroes and heroines
The scholars in the classroom
Provided me with knowledge

The birds' singing on the mulberry
Made me absolutely happy
The wild geese's honking on Charles River
Fitted the pathos in me

终于明白
对于情感
简单
只是一种希冀
复杂
却是一种风景
悲欢离合的演绎
编成人生这出大戏

青涩褪尽
沧桑带来伤情
时日过去
离别悄然临近
不舍的离情
让心生出哀愁的美丽

哀愁诗化了人生
美丽成就了诗意
诗意人生
从此如影随形

2016-03-28，11:29

I finally understand
In terms of feeling
Simple is only a kind of wish
Complicated is a kind of scenery
Life is a big game
Composed of sorrows and happiness
Together with separations and reunions

Youth passed away
Vicissitudes produced sentiments
As time went by
The day of leaving was coming
And wistfulness led to melancholy beauty

To be sorrowful is poetic
And poetry is composed of beauty
My life has ever since
Been accompanied by poetry writing

03/28/2016

13. 白云 · 信笺

你说
三千六百多个时日过去
为什么
对我的思念
还是千丝万缕

我说
时间的推移
不会让爱逝去
只能证明
爱的刻骨铭心

你说
真的希望
此生还有机会
跟我漫步在山林小径
看彩虹飞瀑
听山野鹿鸣

我说
深刻的记忆
一次足矣
任何时候想起
都是一种甜蜜

你说
我们虽属同一方蓝天
却两不相望
只能寄语无边的相思

13. White Clouds and Letter Paper

You say to me
Ten years has passed
But you still miss me so much
And you do not know why

I reply
Time's flying cannot carry away love
It can only prove love is true

You say to me
You really wish that in this life
We could still have the opportunity
To take a walk along the trail
To watch the waterfall
To listen to the belling of the deer

I reply
For impressive memory
Once is enough
Whenever you pick it up
It will give you sweetness

You say to me
We are under the same sky
Yet we can only miss each other
As we cannot get together

I reply
We share the same sun and the moon
This is already endless happiness

我说
共有一个太阳
同沐一片月光
已经享有无尽的幸福

你说
太阳和月亮
还有日月同辉的辉煌
可我和你
除了思念
任何希冀
都是一种绝望的梦想

我说
爱的浪漫
就在心灵的契合
即使不能相见
也没有离开爱的磁场

你说
思念多了
反而想忘却
可是越想忘却
无奈的伤感越强

我说
一切
顺其自然
刻意的挣扎
只会让心更加受伤

You say to me
Even the sun and the moon
Can appear in the sky together sometimes
But what you and I can have
Is only missing
Any yearning is a kind of despair

I reply
The romance of love
Lies in the harmony of two hearts
Though meeting is impossible
Our love is still in the same magnetic field

You say to me
Missing too much
Allures you to think of giving up
But the more you want to forget
The more impressive the memory is

I reply
Just take things as they come
To struggle purposefully
Will only lead to more agony

I know
Every day you ask the wind
To send me a white cloud
With your aspiration and yearning

我知道
每天
你都托风
给我捎来一朵白云
上面写满你的思念

而我
同样以白云为信笺
用诗意的相思
吻合你的思念

天地间
你这颗孤星
陪伴我这个忧伤的月亮
孤星伴月的景致
胜过所有苍白的语言

2016-03-29，9:52

And I
Also use the cloud as the letter paper
To write you a love letter in poetry

In the universe
You are a lonely star
And I am the melancholy moon
As long as you accompany me in the sky
Our love is beyond all languages to describe

03/29/2016

14. 心已回港

心
曾经像纯净的海
没有杂质
一片湛蓝

错愕的际遇
让心迷惘
于是
带着疑惑
不顾一切去流浪

远方的风景
暖阳灿烂
一场撕心裂肺的哭泣
哭痛了心
也洗刷了淤积的迷茫

体味了身旅沧桑
看淡了世态炎凉
终于
让心回到出发的港湾

不再憧憬
即使在梦里
也已不再幻想
太阳西斜的时候
静坐水边
不是冥想
而是闲看夕阳
沐浴最后一缕
属于自己的阳光

2016-04-03, 07:23

14. The Heart Back in the Harbor

My heart used to be so pure
So blue and so clean
Just like the sea

Unfavorable circumstances
Confused my heart so much
That it wandered on earth
Aimlessly and perplexedly

The faraway view
Was splendid though
Which led to a bitter cry
So the accumulated confusion
Was washed away and died

Disappointing human relationships
Together with tiredness
Finally made me decide
To navigate my heart back to the harbor

No more wishing
No more fantasy
Even if in a dream
When the sun is rising
I will just sit at the seaside
Not for meditation
But to watch the sun setting down
And enjoy the last ray of the sunshine

04/03/2016

15. 告白

真的
我的记性不好
而且越来越差
如果一不小心
把你遗忘
也只好请你原谅

心
虽然长在自己身上
却无法控制它的想法
而大脑也在辩白
当今世界
信息量太大
如果不及时清理记忆
一旦内存不足
大脑将会停止运转

你是愿意我大脑呆滞
还是愿意让我遗忘
不要告诉我
你两个都不想
生活
很多时候
选择只有单项

15. Confession

It is true
My memory is poor
And it is getting worse and worse
So it is possible
That I will forget you
Please forgive me
If it happens so

My mind is located in my body
But I just cannot control its thinking
My brain also argues
The world is filled with lots of information
So it has to cancel many memories
In case someday it will stop working

Either to get dementia
Or to forget you
Which one do you prefer
Don't tell me
You will refuse both
In life
Most of the time
You will have to choose

其实

不管你如何选择

结果都是遗忘

过程

比结果美好

回味过程

忘了开始与结束

这

才是生活应有的立场

2016-04-03，08:17

As a matter of fact
The only choice is forgetfulness
As the process is better than the result
The positive attitude towards life
Is to keep the sweet memory
And forget the beginning and ending

04/03/2016

16. 远方的诗意

在远方
坐拥诗意和孤单
对影
也成三人
却不如青莲居士
少了一份狂醉与潇洒

在远方
疏离在此称王
剑河边漫步
也在思考与冥想
结果却总是纠结不断

却有那路边的野花
旁若无人地开放
对着我的镜头
婀娜招展
吻合我心底的期盼

于是
每日与白云为伴
让风吹起心底的柔情
随春天一起勃发

2016-04-04，19:10

16. Poetic Mind Afar

In a faraway country
What I own are poetic mind and solitude
With the moon in the sky
Together with my shadow on the ground
We form a group of three
The great poet Li Bai
Used to be drunk and unrestrained
Which is just what I lack

In a faraway country
Alienation is the king
I stroll along the River Cam
Thinking and meditating
Only to gain tangles in the mind

The wild flowers at the roadside
Blossom regardless of anything
They sway joyfully in the wind
Which arouses my ever-lasting yearning

So every day
I regard the clouds as my company
And let the wind soothe my feeling
So as to keep my heart with the spring

04/04/2016

17. 月的回想

树梢的月亮
清冷而芬芳
独坐窗前
默默对月
情不自禁地回想

那一年
寂寥而孤单
因心伤而不顾一切北上
与月邂逅
在泰山脚下
一场痛哭
洗尽所有的忧伤

如洗的月光
披洒在旷野之上
月影西斜
填埋了我的痛楚
我终究还是败了
却也败得不失浪漫

这以后
在月下
总是禁不住回望
来时的路
已然荒芜
曾经的心
却还在流浪
天堂
不是归宿
魂归处
唯有旷野中温柔的月光

2016-04-06，21:53

17. Recollections in the Moonlight

The moon perches on the tree
Glorious and chilly
At the window alone I am sitting
And looking at the moon
Recollections burst from the inside of me

In that very year
I was lonely and gloomy
In order to avoid agony
I took a northward journey
And met the moon
At the foot of Mount Tai
I cried bitterly
Letting the tears wash away my misery

The mellow moonlight
Streamed on the wilderness
When the moon went westward
It carried away my distress
Yes, I was a loser
But a loser with romance

Ever since then
Whenever in the moonlight
I cannot help looking back
The road I have taken
Is already deserted
But my heart is still wandering
As the paradise is not home
I'd rather end up
In the mellow moonlight

04/06/2016

18. 隐约的牵挂

就像梅雨季节偶见的晴天
就像冬日里盛开的鲜花
对你的思念
只是一种隐约的牵挂

大多数日子
总是把你淡忘
可是
夜深无眠时
就会想起你的影像
心情烦忧时
就会想起你的诗行

隐约的牵挂
无人知晓的情感
面对你
牵挂丝毫不露
反而对你苛严有加

也曾在内心挣扎
劝自己放弃这种情感
可挣扎无果
最终只能顺其自然

不想告诉你
却希望你能知晓
可我知道
这种灵犀
只是一种奢望

18. *Slight Concern*

The slight concern
Is a faint yearning for you
It is an exceptionally rare feeling
Just like the sunny days in the rainy season
And the flowers in chilly winter

Most of the days
I put you at the back of my mind
But deep into the night
I cannot help missing you
And when I feel unhappy
I will always think of your poetry

No one understands this concern
Which is hidden safely in my mind
When I see you
No clue of it is ever shown
What I do instead
Is to pretend to be cold to you

I often struggle with myself
Persuading myself to give up the concern
Struggles turn out to be in vain
And I have to take it for granted

I don't want to tell you about it
Yet I wish you could sense it
Though I know quite well
That the wish is only a wild one

我只能把这种牵挂
放在心灵深处
这个地方
即使我自己的心
也只能偶尔前往

隐约的牵挂
真实而渺茫
可我甘愿被缚
因为
就这缥缈的思念
已经给了我无尽的快感

2016-04-08，10:01

I can only put this concern
At the bottom of my heart
Even I myself will visit there
Only once in a while

The slight concern
Is true yet uncertain
I am willing to be bound to it
As this faint yearning
Has already brought endless happiness to me

04/08/2016

19. 向晚的暮色

向晚
暮色苍茫
笼罩了一切
却遮挡不了绚丽的晚霞

教堂的尖顶
沐浴着霞光
那一片柔光下
疑是天堂所在的地方

在这一方土地上
无数的亚当和夏娃
却还在泥沼中挣扎
为了生计
为了名利
也为了虚无缥缈的情感

空中
墨云涌动
彩云相伴
大自然的一切
相对于人类
总是那么潇洒而浪漫

暮色中的古木
高大而挺拔
见证着人类与自然的变迁
却始终一言不发

19. Twilight at Dusk

At dusk
Twilight is deepening
Everything gets dim
Except the gorgeous rosy beams

The spire of the church
Is bathed in the glow
Where the tender light emits
Is supposed to be the paradise

In this world
Countless Adams and Eves
Are struggling in the bog
For making a living
For fame and money
And also for the illusory feeling

The black clouds
Are swarming in the sky
Accompanied by the rosy clouds
Everything in nature
Compared with human beings
Is unrestrained and romantic

The old trees
Tall and straight
Witness the vicissitudes of Man and nature
But they always keep silent

暮色裹挟着我
在微风中徜徉
悟人类之渺小
静静地膜拜
大自然无形的力量

2016-04-08，10:33

I also bathe myself in the twilight
And stroll freely in the breeze
I then realize
How insignificant the human beings are
And silently worship nature's unseen force

04/08/2016

20. 缘来缘去

缘
是冥冥中的定数
来时如风
去时如雨

缘来时
挡也挡不住
即使相隔万里
也要相约而聚

缘去时
连告别也已经多余
两人背道而行
渐行渐远
直到最后
互相忘记

缘
来无因
去无果
缘来缘去
不过是人生的花絮

是故
缘来时无须狂喜
缘去时无须唏嘘
缘来时惜缘
缘去时别缘
只要心有定力
生活便永远精彩而绚丽

2016-04-09，10:26

20. Karma Comes and Goes

Karma is fateful
It comes quietly like wind
It goes suddenly like rain

When it comes
Nothing can stop it
Dating is inevitable
Though the lovers
Are far away from each other

When it goes
Farewell is unnecessary
The lovers follow different directions
With a longer and longer distance in between
Until they forget each other completely

Karma
Comes without any reason
And leaves without any result
It comes and goes
Which is just sidelight of life

Therefore
When karma comes
Don't lose yourself with happiness
When it goes
Don't lament on its sudden loss
Cherish it when it comes
And say goodbye when it goes
As long as you are determined
Life will always be colorful

04/09/2016

21. 远方的诗和心里的画

沐着阳光
耽溺于无谓的冥想
我的生活有诗和远方
而我的远方
有你和思念
一如既往

曾经
那是一片蛮荒
我困惑
你迷茫
当你我不期然相遇
心光
点亮了时光隧道的火种
黑暗隐退
青绿昭然
蛮荒
成了传说中的伊甸园
到处洒满金色的阳光

如今
我在这里
你在远方
你作为诗的形象
伫立在水边
让我的诗意
源源不断

21. Faraway Poetry and Painting

In the sunshine
I indulge in useless thinking
In my life
I am engaged in composing poetry
At the same time
I look forward to the faraway country
Where you live with ever-lasting yearning

We used to be in the foreworld
I was confused and you were perplexed
When we met unexpectedly
The heart light
Ignited the kindling in the time tunnel
The fire drove away the darkness
And brought about greenery
Thus the foreworld turned out to be Eden
Filled with the golden sunshine

Now I am here
While you are faraway
As an image of poetry
You stand at the waterside
Providing me with limitless poetic thinking

These poems
Do not need readers
In every one of them
You are the only image
And every word
Having been attuned by your heart
Is the spontaneous flow of feeling

这些诗行
已经不需要读者
每一首诗
你都是唯一的意象
而每一个字
都经过你心的点化
这些
都是自然流露的情感

是的
自然
便是万事万物存在的理由
唯其如此
你才成了我远方的诗
和用心情涂鸦的画

诗画人生
写意自然
诗和远方
成就诗意的
秋和冬
春与夏
此生
不再枉然

2016-04-10, 8:08

Yes
Being natural
Is the reason of survival
Just because of this
You have become my poetry afar
And a painting painted by my heart

Poetic life and pleasant nature
Lead to poetry and yearning
All these make the poetic seasons
Spring and summer
Autumn and winter
And thus my life is not in vain

04/10/2016

22. 暮年时分

暮年时分
只想和你坐在这里
看芦苇摇曳
听树间风吟

孩提时
我们顽皮嬉戏
青年时
我们挥霍年轻
中年时
我们闲坐小憩
现在
耄耋之年
我们蹒跚在苇间小径
闲看白云飘荡
感叹白驹过隙

沉默
是我们常态的语言
没有尴尬
不觉孤寂
只有你知我知
无须打破的静谧

风吟依旧
鸟鸣嘤嘤
从我的白发间
你看到了青葱岁月
从你的皱纹里
我读出了共有的曾经

2016-04-10，21:49

22. When We Are Old

When we are old
I only want to sit here with you
Watching the reeds dancing in the wind
And listening to the wind blowing in the forest

In childhood
We were naughty and played vigorously
In youth
We wasted time fearing nothing
In middle age
We gradually slowed down our paces
Now
When we are old
We stroll down the trail in the reeds
Looking at the clouds in the sky
And lamenting on the time's flying

Silence is our everyday language
But we are not embarrassed and solitary
As both you and I
Know this appropriate tranquility

The wind is blowing
While the birds are singing
In my grey hair
You see the past youth
And in your wrinkles
I read our shared experience

04/10/2016

23. 顺其自然

拉开窗帘
迎进阳光
看春意萌发
观云海变幻

景色宜人
伴随追风的过程
亲眼所见
就是收获
又何必在乎生命的短长

已知的已然已知
未知的继续未知
就算未知要伺机而动
带来灾难
在心震来临之前
且让心无忧无虑
继续沉醉于诗和远方

随劲风狂吹
伴细雨飘洒
在剑桥的风雨中
思考生死的命相

追风的过程
结束只在早晚
早
不失为一种幸福
晚
未尝就是一种圆满

23. *Play It as It Lays*

I pull the curtain aside
To welcome the sunlight
The clouds are displayed in front of me
Together with the spring

The splendid view
Accompanies my life journey
Of chasing the wind
To witness is to gain
Whether the lifespan is short or long
Is not important at all

Those known to all are already known
Those unknown remain to be unknown
Even though the unknown
Are to bring about disasters
Before they come
Just feel carefree
And cling to romance and poetry

With strong wind bellowing
And light rain drizzling
I ponder over life and death
In beautiful Cambridge

The activity of chasing the wind
Will end sooner or later
The sooner
The more happiness you will gain
The later
The more misery you will obtain

徒然的挣扎
无谓的妄想
徒增恼人的惆怅

告诫自己
不论何时何地
步入既定的轨道
顺其自然地运转

2016-04-14, 16:16

Vain struggles and fantasy
Only lead to irritating melancholy

I just tell myself
Whenever it is and wherever I am
I will follow the destined orbit
And move as naturally as I can

04/14/2016

24. 困扰

问题
困扰于心
梦里
百般缠结
无解

脆弱
如春之新绿
不堪一击

曾经如麋鹿
不知疲倦地奔跑
身之英姿
羡煞路人
自信
了然于胸

往事如烟
太阳升起
梦境退去
新的一天
困扰依旧

2016-04-16，08:16

24. *Obsession*

My heart is obsessed with problems
And in the dream
I cannot find solutions

As fragile as the early green
I will collapse at the first blow of attacking

I used to be an elk
Always running tirelessly
Confidence was everywhere in my body
Even the passersby admired me surprisingly

Past is past
The sun also rises
The dream fades
The new day comes
Yet
I am still obsessed with problems

04/16/2016

25. 剑桥的雨

没有瓢泼
没有倾盆
唯有绵绵细雨
永远淅淅沥沥

纵有丁香姑娘的幽怨
也无法撑着油纸伞慢行
剑桥的雨
在风的裹挟下
只容与你零距离

剑桥的雨
温婉而细腻
打不下满地残红
却催发无限春意

当雨丝飘落眉梢
雨意凉透心里
遏止不住的思念
随细雨弥漫天际

2016-04-16，13:30

25. The Rain at Cambridge

Not heavy
Not pouring
Only light rain
Always drizzling

Though Lady Lilac is melancholy
She cannot hold her umbrella and walk slowly
The rain at Cambridge
Blown by the wind
Keeps distance with nobody

It is mild and soft
Though too weak to destroy the flowers
It urges spring to come early

When the rain kisses my brow
And the coolness touches my heart
The uncontrollable yearning for you
Diffuses into the sky with drizzling

04/16/2016

26. 夜晚

夜晚
关上窗扉
让自己的影子
陪伴自己

不是失眠症患者
却也失去了耐心
夜的黑
拉开了有眠与无眠的距离

希冀无言自通的灵犀
却总是收获无心
剑河的水
即使不起涟漪
也比无心人有情

隐约的相思
已然无影
孤独症患者
在大自然中迤逦独行
侧耳倾听
只有自然母亲的心音

夜晚
主动拉开与你的距离
其实
背道而行
亦不失为一种浪漫之举

2016-04-16，21:46

26. *At Night*

At night
I close the window
To let myself
Only accompanied by my own shadow

Not suffering from insomnia
I also get impatient
The darkness at night
Makes difference between sleeping and waking

Longing for a silent understanding
Only to find a false feeling
Water in the River Cam
Even if in tranquility
Is more affectionate than the human being

The slight concern
Is nowhere to earn
Suffering from autism
I take solitary walks in nature
Listening to the heart beat of Mother Earth

At night
I quietly keep a distance from you
As a matter of fact
To follow different directions
Is also a kind of action of romance

04/16/2016

27. 婆娑的心情

春日的暖阳
滤出无数的光
光影
在剑河的水面扑朔迷离

婆娑的光影
揉进剑河的波里
光波
荡出醉人的涟漪

河畔的树
投影在水里
婆娑的树影
光怪陆离
营造缠绵的意境

是何造物
离间了浪漫的诗意
未知带来忐忑
忐忑疏离了爱情

没有爱的远方
诗意流落天涯
当阳光隐去
雨丝淅沥
坠落一片
婆娑的心情

2016-04-17, 11:13

27. *Whirling Feeling*

The warm sun in spring
Lets out countless beams
They dance on the River Cam
Whirling and confusing

The whirling beams
Merge into the water
And stir up ripples intoxicatingly

Trees at the riverbank
Reflect in the water
The whirling shadows
Lustrous and dazzling
Produce moving poetic imagery

What exactly
Destroys romantic sense
The unknown leads to uncertainty
And in turn alienates the love story

In a faraway place
Where love is missing
Poetic flavor is in exile
When the sunshine fades
And the rain drizzles in the sky
What is left in me
Is only a whirling feeling

04/17/2016

28. 傍晚的月亮

不等太阳落山
东天边上
出现了半个月亮
苍白的脸
面露忧伤
是不忍与太阳告别
抑或是还有别的忧烦

望月
望出了无尽的伤感
我的心
如剑河的水
划艇的桨
一下
又一下
划乱了惯有的静
划出了未曾有过的凄怆

诗情与浪漫
如满地落花
金柳垂泪
散发无人知晓的颓丧

忧伤的月亮
吻合我心底的悲凉
淡淡的愁
变成了汹涌的浪

28. The Moon at Dusk

Before the sun sets down
Half a moon appears on the eastern sky
Pale and melancholy
It seems reluctant
To say goodbye to the sun
Or obsessed with other agonies

Looking at the moon
Leads to endless sentiments
My heart
Like the water in the River Cam
Is disturbed by the oars
Tranquility is missing
And what arrives is only misery

Poetic flavor and romance
Go away like fallen flowers
The golden willows are still weeping
With the unknown frustration spreading

The melancholy moon
Meets the sadness in my heart
Then
The gloomy mood overwhelms me
Like the roaring waves in the sea

沉浮间
一切已经消亡
唯有树梢的月亮
怆然而泪下

2016-04-17，23:14

Rocking up and down
Everything goes to nothingness
Only the moon
Hiding in the tree
Sheds tears sadly for everything

04/17/2016

29. 逃亡

憧憬
敌不过现实的无情
盼来了春意
却带不走沉重的凄清

逃亡
以胜利者的姿态
或许
前路布满荆棘
没有选择
唯有带着勇敢者的面具
迈步前行

淡定
总是能退敌千里
心理的天平
放上自信的砝码
陪伴天涯之孤旅

2016-04-18，08:57

29. Running away

Hope
Cannot fight with ruthlessness
Though spring finally comes
It cannot drive away the heavy loneliness

Running away
Not as a loser but as a winner
Though the road is full of thorns and thistles
I will go forward with courage

Serenity
Will always drive back the enemy
Psychological balance with confidence
Will go side by side with the lonely journey

04/18/2016

30. 不确定

冷暖没有了规律
四季不再分明
一切不可预知
知道了
却无能为力
不确定
成了后现代社会的特性

天不确定
地不确定
人不确定
事
同样也不确定

未知的忐忑
似春蚕食桑
总在噬咬意欲平静的心

于是
心乱了
有了错位的情感
身乱了
暴发各种疾病

那么
不妨让神经也错乱吧
疯了
躲进自己的躯壳
那里有一种幸福
也有一份宁静

2016-04-20，20:17

30. Uncertainty

The weather is always changing
Seasons are in obscurity
Everything is unpredictable
And uncertainty
Becomes the characteristic
Of the postmodern society

The sky lies in uncertainty
The earth lies in uncertainty
Human beings are in uncertainty
And events are also in uncertainty

The unknown fact
Disturbs the balance of mentality
The heart
Expecting calmness
Is bitten bit and bit
Just like the silkworms
Which are nipping the mulberry leaves

Therefore
The heart is in discomposure
Which leads to the dislocated feeling
And the body is unhealthy
Which results in various diseases

Then
Let insanity dominate the body
In insanity
There is a kind of happiness
And also special tranquility

04/20/2016

31. 陌生化

从身与身的零距离
到心与心的远隔千里
不经意间
成就了多少风景
又塑造了多少疏离

再见你
已然是隔世的记忆
我苦思冥想
依旧找不到曾经的交集

你说
你很难想象
我居然会把你忘记
我愕然
因为我一直以为
这就是你想要的结局

你说
我一点都不明白你的心
我默然
因为在我心里
你就是个深不见底的谜

如今
多年过去
你神秘依旧
可我已经失去
揭开谜底的兴趣

31. Alienation

Once
There was no distance between you and me
But now your heart
Is far away from mine
From then to the present
We have created many splendid views
As well as a lot of alienation

When I see you again
There is only memory from centuries ago
I think and think and think
Still I cannot find our shared experience

You say to me
You cannot imagine
You have been erased from my memory
I am startled and confused
As I always think
It is exactly what you want as an ending

You say to me
I do not understand you at all
I just keep silent
As you always remain
An unfathomable enigma to me

So many years has passed
You are still mysterious
But I have already lost my interest
In solving the mystery

在心底异化你
陌生替代了熟悉
牵挂变成了忘记

以牵引开始
以忘记结束
既然我已经先你而行
还是请你
从此把我忘记

2016-04-23，10:23

I have alienated you in my heart
Strangeness takes the place of familiarity
Concern gradually becomes forgetfulness

Love between you and me
Began with attraction
And ended with forgetfulness
As I have already forgotten you
Please do your best to forget me

04/23/2016

32. 水草的自白

枝繁叶茂时
你为我遮风挡雨
柔弱的我
因此免除了诸多艰辛

落叶时
你和我相守相依
共同沐浴阳光
一起承受风雨
我用我的柔弱之躯
为你增添有限的绿意

只要我在你身边
你便永远还有生命
枯萎
不是死的象征
而是爱的开始
我们伫立水边
和谐而默契

跨越死生界的藩篱
超越有限的生命
我和你
永远站在这里
生时不离
死亦不弃

2016-04-29，08:44

32. *Confessions of the Waterplant*

When you are in your prime
You protect me from the rain and wind
Weak as me
I then am exempt from misery

When you are withering
You are still accompanying me
We share the sunshine
And we stand against the rain and wind
Though I am weak
I provide you with the limited green

As long as I am side by side with you
Your life is forever prolonged
To wither
Is not the sign of death
But the beginning of love
We stand at the waterside
Harmoniously and happily

We will cross the line
Between life and death
And defeat mortality
You and I
Will forever stand here together
Both in this life and after death

04/29/2016

33. 脆弱的年龄

脆弱的年龄
一切了然无序
中心不再凝聚
规律已然无迹

脆弱的年龄
睡眠也成了一种病
眼皮困顿不已
心却异常清醒

脆弱的年龄
身心已然分离
身力渐弱的时候
心力一片空虚

脆弱的年龄
如秀于林的木
风过处
摧枯拉朽
枝叶满地

脆弱的年龄
犹如秋末的最后一片黄叶
孤独地抵挡冬日的来临

这片叶里
透出一股顽强的心力
静静的等待中
姿态依然优美
决绝已然淡定

33. *Weak Age*

In weak age
Everything is messy
The center cannot hold
Rules are nowhere to see

In weak age
Sleeping is a kind of illness
When sleepiness falls on the eyelids
The mind is still working

In weak age
The body departs from the mind
When the body is unhealthy
The heart is lonely and empty

In weak age
The body is like the tallest tree
In the forest
When a gust of strong wind blows over
The tree loses all its leaves
Which fall down and crackle on the ground

The weak age
Is like the last yellow leaf in autumn
Trying to fight against winter solitarily

This last leaf
Posing elegantly and calmly
Displays a force of the mind

当那阵风终于来临
叶在风中飘落
留下一生无悔的记忆

2016-05-01，9∶36

When the expected wind finally comes
It floats down to the earth
With unregretful memories

05/01/2016

34. 心的化石

于车水马龙中
寻求一份心的宁静
让思绪摒除噪音
进入思维的禁地

很多联系
渐渐趋于平静
想起时
只能用淡然的笑
再次尘封曾经的记忆

孤独
是人类始终如一的状态
所谓的心有灵犀
只是瞬间的感觉
所谓的心心相印
只是人们的希冀

在喧嚣的尘世里
离析一份特有的孤寂
吻合山的空鸣
水的静谧
风的低吟
雨的淅沥

心
从此成了化石

2016-05-01，12：00

34. The Fossilized Heart

I try to find heart's tranquility
In a flow of heavy traffic
Letting my mind get rid of the noise
And enter the world of meditating

Many relations
Tend to be silent gradually
When I recall all these
I can only smile indifferently
And put them at the back of my memory

Solitude is the ordinary state
Of the human being
From beginning to the end
The so-called mutual understanding
Is only temporary
The so-called deep affinity
Is only a kind of wishing

In the clamorous world
I try to isolate myself
To be in tune with
The bellowing of the mountains
The tranquility of the water
The singing of the wind
And the falling of the raindrops

The heart
Is then fossilized

05/01/2016

35. 孤鸟的哀鸣

穿透清晨的凄清
你奋力啼鸣
悲怆凄厉
引发了众鸟齐鸣

然而
它们并非应和你
叽叽喳喳的声音
不是安慰
自然也不是同情

不久以后
当城市完全苏醒
你的啼鸣
也将被喧嚣淹没
再也无人能听到
你痛苦的哀啼

其实
就算每个清晨
不止一人听到你的鸣叫
多数人只是嫌你噪聒
惊扰了他们的梦境
又有几人能理解你
从你的悲鸣里
听出痛苦与孤寂

35. *The Whine of the Lonely Bird*

In the solitude of the early morning
You are whining
Loudly, pathetically and plaintively
Which results in the chorus of all birds

However
They are not echoing your whine
The noise of chirping and twittering
Is neither consolation nor sympathy

Shortly after the whole city wakes up
Your whine will be subdued by the clamor
No one can then hear your sorrowful crying

In fact
In every early morning
Though many people hear your whine
Most of them just complain
You are too noisy and annoying
Waking them up from their dream
How many of them
Can sense from your whine
The solitude and misery

It is similar to the human being
If you amount to something
You will win suspicion and envy
If you achieve nothing
You will only gain scorn and disdain

一如人类
有了成绩
则招来怨恨、猜疑和妒忌
平庸无为
却让人不屑和瞧不起

身痛苦时
病菌的折磨犹在其次
更难忍受的
是仇者的幸灾乐祸
心痛苦时
不敢奢望共鸣
还被说成是无病呻吟

不能多思
思考本身就是深渊
再痛苦
也只能独自承受
一如孤鸟的悲鸣
于己是一种表达
于人则是一种打扰
邻人们
恨不得赶走这只孤鸟
复归清晨死一般的寂静

孤鸟的悲鸣
吻合我心底怆然的心绪
任何时候
任何地方
悲凉是序曲
孤寂是主题
虚无
则是恒久不变的结局

2016-05-04，12:24

When in illness
The misery resulted from the bacteria
Is not so unbearable as the enemy's pleasure
When in agony
Understanding is only a wild wish
People will only say
You just groan out of nothing

Don't think
Thinking itself is a chasm of agony
Miserable as I am
I can only stand it alone and lonely
Just as the whine of the lonely bird
It is a kind of expression for itself
While a disturbance to others
People in the neighborhood
Are eager to drive it away
So that the early morning
Can go back to deadly quietness again

The whine of the lonely bird
Echoes the sorrow in my heart
Whenever it is
Wherever I am
Forlornness is the overture
Solitude is the theme
And nothingness
Is the permanent ending

05/04/2016

36. 晚春的风

起风了
风吹皱了水面
也吹折了身心

风带来缕缕寒意
替代了晚春的生机
是否
夏天还未到来
秋天却已经逼近

最喜欢的季节
却是离别的前夕
冬的严寒
摧毁一切
是谁在幻想
冬也在孕育来年的生命

结束便结束了
此生已已
便不希冀来世
无悔
无怨
无情

2016-05-04，18:43

36. The Wind in Late Spring

The wind is rising
The water in the river ripples
And the heart is upset

Coolness brought about by the wind
Takes the place of vitality in late spring
Is it that
Autumn is eager to approach
Before summer is in the scene

Farewell has to be said
In my favorite season
The coldness in winter
Will destroy everything
It is only illusion
That winter will breed
The life of the following year

Past is past
That is the end of this life
No need to cherish hope for afterlife
No regrets
No complaints
No more illusion in love

05/04/2016

37. 我，是一座孤岛

我
是一座孤岛

这座孤岛
没有稀有的富矿
成不了利益的工场
没有旖旎的风光
招不来游人的目光
没有瓜果飘香
成就不了桃花源的幻想

这座孤岛
没有沃土
没有森林
唯有嶙峋的怪石
遍布岛的四面八方

世人眼里
这是一座荒岛
不
比荒还糟
简直就是死岛
占着地球的一角
却没有任何回报

可我
不善于伪装
始终展示自己的原生态

37. I Am a Desolate Island

I am
A desolate island

On this island
There is no rich ore
Which is able to produce substantial profit
There is no beautiful scenery
Which can attract tourists
There is no orchard with fruits
Which is similar to the Garden of Eden

On this island
There is neither futile soil nor forest
Only the jagged rocks everywhere
Are the masters of the land

In ordinary people's eyes
It is desolate
Or even worse
It is a dead island on the earth
Incapable of producing anything

However
I cannot pretend to be another land
Instead of being what I am

嶙峋的怪石
筑成一道天然的风景
巨石碎浪
尽显大自然的威力
浪花击石
无怨无悔
那份决绝与潇洒
总是被浪涛谱成雄浑的乐章
在岛的四周恒久鸣唱

这座岛
不需要无良的开发
不需要虚伪的夸赞
不需要浅薄的访客
不需要垂怜的目光

这座岛
独一无二
孤而不傲
以本真的面目示人
一如既往

2016-05-07，10:30

The jagged rocks
Can also make a natural landscape
The waves break upon the rocks
Showing the force of nature
With no regrets and complaints
Their determination and freedom
Are composed into melody
So that the island
Is filled with music permanently

This island
Needs neither unscrupulous development
Nor hypocritical compliments
Nor superficial visitors
Nor sympathetic admiration

This island is unique
Desolate yet not arrogant
It shows its originality and sincerity
In the past
At present
And in the future

05/07/2016

38. 梦

狂风大作
飞沙走石
祥和的溪浣图
转瞬即逝

山雨欲来
危险四伏
遍寻避难之所
只有一处庙宇
却山门紧闭
不管不顾

尘缘未了
凡心太重
在污浊的尘世沉浮
无所谓出世入世

2016-05-08，07:50

38. Dream

A fierce gale springs up
Throwing sands and pebbles in all directions
The happy scene of washing at the riverside
Disappears in an instant

A storm is approaching
And danger lurks on every side
I look for a shelter everywhere
But only find a temple in the mountain
Its gate is closed
And it remains indifferent

Having links with the mortal life
I feel reluctant to abandon this world
Though living in the chaotic society
I feel unable to detach from it

05/08/2016

39. 在你的心里开放

我
在你的心里开放
不但让自己更美
也促你更加色彩斑斓

我并非选择了你
只是心在徜徉时
遇见了你的心
从此认定
这便是我的沃土

你毫不犹豫接受了我
因为你意识到
我
就是你多年耐心等候的
那朵独一无二的花

2016-05-11, 8:12

39. I Blossom in You

I blossom in you
So much so that
I not only beautify myself
But also better you

I do not choose you
I just encounter you
When my heart is wandering
I then decide immediately
You are the very field for me

You accept me without hesitation
Realizing that I am the very peculiar flower
After years of your patient waiting

05/11/2016

40. 夜半随想

夜半
鬼魅横生
睡意催眠了众生
遗漏夜半游魂

痛感
占领了每一根神经
细胞毫无睡意
奢侈地消耗生命

这个时候
纵想揽点浪漫
夜色却不再温柔
与静交织在一起
死一般
是唯一的词语

纵是考验
已然过了期限
只想最后的结果
要么凯旋
要么告别一切
可是
为什么
总是这么悬而未决

2016-05-14，02:26

40. *Midnight Thinking*

At midnight
Ghosts are still wandering
Sleepiness drives living creatures into dream
Leaving behind some souls loitering

Pain occupies every nerve
The cells cannot go to sleep
Wasting the precious time extravagantly

At this time of the night
Though you want to be romantic
The night is not so cooperative
It mingles with tranquility
Making deadly the only suitable word
To modify everything

Even if it is a test
It has exceeded the time limit
Only the final result is expected
Victory or farewell
But the thorny thing is that
There is always only uncertainty

05/14/2016

41. 相思花

属于你的季节
你毫不犹豫地绽放
漫山遍野
肆无忌惮
浪漫
自此在空中弥漫

曾经执着于一份幻想
把相思当成生命的奇葩
植在心里
用心浇灌
默默观赏
希冀相思永恒
长此以往

然而
世上没有不凋零的花
当花儿萎谢
相思成了无谓的情感
终于明白
不对等的相思
无异于慢性自杀

心
从此豁然
流放相思
放弃牵挂
在相思花开的季节
依旧赏花
却不再耽溺于
相思的虚幻

2016-05-15, 08:56

41. Acacia Flower

In your season
You blossom without hesitation
Over the mountains
You produce romance
Which pervades the universe

Once sticking to a kind of illusion
I regarded yearning for you
As an exotic flower in my life
I planted it in my heart
And watered it carefully
I also admired its beauty in silence
Wishing this yearning
Would last permanently

However
Flowers in this world always wither
And yearning has become useless feeling
I finally realized
Unequal yearning was actually slow suicide

I was suddenly enlightened
So I exiled the yearning for you
And gave up the concerns
When acacia flowers blossom again
I still admire them
But never indulge myself in any illusion

05/15/2016

42. 怨随风逝，心随云飘

不管有什么遭际
生活一如往昔
不需要什么救世主
天还是一样湛蓝
云还是一样飘逸

久未造访的草地
依旧青绿如昔
未开的花儿
已绽开花蕾
窥探若有似无的春意

心情如流水
每天都在更新
逝者确实如斯
沿途的风景
却已丰富了人生的阅历

怨
随风而逝
心
随云而飘
幸福痛苦
成功失败
不过都是过眼烟云
倏忽间
了无踪影

2016-05-16，08:32

42. *Grudge Goes with the Wind*

Under any circumstance
Life is the same as always
The savior is not required
The sky is as blue as ever
And the clouds are as free as usual

The grassland is as green as before
Though I haven't visited it for a long time
The flowers are in buds
Peering on the early spring

The mood is like running water
It never becomes stagnant
Things flow away every day
And the scenery on the way
Has enriched the life experience

Grudge
Goes with the wind
The mood
Flies with the clouds
Happiness or agony
Success or failure
All are just passing clouds
Which will disappear without any trace

05/16/2016

43. 奈若何

虚弱之躯
如一片黄叶
抵挡不住任何风雨

力薄如蝼蚁
居然闯入未知的禁区
医学乏术
羞赧地表达诚挚的歉意

无奈在延续
没有尽头
此时此刻
一切
与我无关

并非我主动放弃
只是虚弱的手
已经无力握住
哪怕一点点时光

2016-05-17，23:40

43. What's To Be Done

The body
Weak as a withering leaf
Cannot withstand any storm

Weak and feeble as an ant
I even intrude
On the unknown no-go area
Medicine is of no use
And can only embarrassedly apologize

No alternative available
And agony prevails
Right at this moment
I have nothing to do with anything

It is not that I give up actively
But that my hands are too weak
To hold onto the time's flowing

05/17/2016

44. 连锁反应

身若伤了
心岂能不伤
岁月虽然静好
人却并非安然无恙

无非过客
又何曾想过成为雕像
没有生命的恒久
于己
全然没有意义
于人
又怎能驻留心里

灿烂如烟花
震耳如爆竹
哗众却不能取宠
何如白云
悠悠千载
悄然飘过
却承揽了无数人的心绪

睹物
岂止是伤情
还有伤身和伤心
冥冥之中
来到天际
祭奠一个尚未离世的魂灵

2016-05-18，07:47

44. *Chain Reaction*

If the body is unhealthy
How can the heart beat normally
Days are rather quiet
But health is not always good

Just a passing traveller in the life journey
I never expect to become a statue to anybody
Eternity without life
To me is nothing
To others
It cannot reside in memory

Fireworks are splendid
And firecrackers are deafening
Though they can attract attention
They cannot get people's favor
However
The everlasting white clouds in the sky
Floating in the air freely and leisurely
Have won countless people's admiration

Seeing the things
Not only leads to sadness
But also trauma in the body
As well as sorrow in heart
Somehow
I just go to the horizon
And mourn a live soul on the mountain

05/18/2016

45. 没有我的日子, 你还好吗?

没有我的日子
你还好吗

你说
我是你平淡生活中
偶尔的惊喜
在你的心海深处
荡起醉人的涟漪
由此引发诗意的激情
带给你无限的快意

没有我的日子
你还好吗

你说
如果你的生活
出现连续的阴雨
我便是偶尔出现的晴天
天光亮时
阴霾尽扫
你的心海
自此平静如镜
任由心帆航行

没有我的日子
你还好吗

45. *Are You OK Without Me*

Are you OK without me

You say to me
In your ordinary life
I am a surprise to you occasionally
Stirring up ripples in your heart sea
And bringing to you poetic passion
And endless happiness

Are you OK without me

You say to me
If it rains continually in your life
I am a rare sunny day to see
When the day breaks up
It is not cloudy at all
You can sail forward in your heart sea
Which is calm and glassy

Are you OK without me

You say to me
After a day's hard work
You always make a cup of tea
And light a cigarette
In so doing
Yearning is merging into the smoke
And your world is filled with happiness

你说
繁杂工作之后
你总是泡上一杯香茗
点燃一支香烟
闲适地品着茶
悠闲地吐着烟圈
思念
便随着烟雾缭绕
弥漫着你的世界

没有我的日子
你还好吗

你说过
你对我的思念
你无法遏止
而我不能拒绝
更无法控制
无论我到哪里
你的思念
定会如影随形

没有我的日子
你还好吗

我似乎看见
你扬起嘴角
微微一笑
说
看来
你对我
并非像你所说
那么不在意

2016-06-17, 07:17

120

Are you OK without me

You say to me
You cannot control your yearning for me
Neither can I refuse and prevent it
Wherever I go
Your concern for me will go with me

Are you OK without me

I seemingly see
A faint smile plays round your lips
Saying that actually I also care for you
Though I often say
That you are nothing to me

06/17/2016

46. 时光 · 古墙

往事
在时空中尘封
时空
在历史中穿行

一扇门
穿过了多少故事
一扇窗
开启了多少风景

一堵堵古墙
刻录了多少沧桑
一丛丛野草
尽显了多少潇洒

时空的某一点
定格了一个影像
不想成为时光的雕像
只想留些故事
在耄耋之年
回味往昔美好的时光

2016-06-23，12:08

46. Time and Ancient Walls

The bygones
Are buried in time and space
Time and space
Travel through history

How many stories
Are witnessed by the door
How many views
Are let in by the window

The ancient walls
Have written many vicissitudes
The wild grasses
Have displayed much peacefulness

At a certain moment in time
And a certain point in space
An image has been established
Not in order to become a statue in time
But to leave some stories behind
To dwell on in old age

06/23/2016

47. 凋谢 · 无悔

该灿烂时
绝不内敛
该凋谢时
绝不留恋
这
便是我的宣言

无意争艳
那是我的本色
娇媚可人
与惜花者结缘

花期既过
落便落了
无悔
是我永恒的姿态
却给人留下
一地的惋惜与眷恋

2016-06-23，14:07

47. Unregretful Withering

As a flower
When I can bloom
I do not refrain from display
When I have to wither
I do not feel reluctant to leave
These are my proclamations

Not competing for beauty in spring
I just bloom
Because it is my nature
I am sweet and charming
Just to please flower lovers

As the season is over
I am ready to wither
To be unregretful is always my attitude
Though I will leave pity and laments
To human beings

06/23/2016

48. 未至的慰藉

夏至虽至
寒而未休的冷意
逼走了夏日的热情
阳光依旧灿烂
却暗藏隐隐的恶意

终于还是抵挡无力
病毒进入躯体
肆虐得登峰造极

我气息奄奄
眼神呆滞
唯有竖起耳朵
辨识你的声音

你的话语
虽不是绵绵情话
却总能给我慰藉
带来某种温情

这是精神的安慰
也是遥远的灵犀

然而
我听到了风声
听到了云吟
甚至听到了
太阳中黑子在爆裂
可你的声音
却始终毫无影迹

2016-07-06, 10:21

48. *Expected Consolation*

Though the Summer Solstice has come
The coldness still lingers on
Summer's passion is driven away
And a kind of indistinct malice
Lurks in the splendid sunshine

Self-protection is in vain
The viruses enter the body
And make the whole body messy

I am at death's door
My eyes are sluggish
I prick up my ears
To sense your voice

Though not sweet words
Your talks can bring consolation to me
Signifying a kind of tender feeling

This is consolation in mentality
And also faraway understanding

However
I have heard the wind's blowing
And the cloud's floating
Even the cracking of the sunspots
But your voice
Is nowhere to hear

07/06/2016

49. 忘尘园

礼堂 雪松 草地
静谧
是唯一的主题

情不自禁地
放轻了步履
交谈变成低语
心灵涤荡了积郁
烦忧竞相远离

忘尘园
遗忘尘世喧嚣
颐养天年知性
身在尘世
心
已绝尘归去

2016-07-08，07:23

49. *Serenity Garden*

The Lee Hall
The cedars
And the grassland
Tranquility is the only theme of all

We walk softly
Lowering our voice to whisper
Accumulated melancholy is driven away
And frets gradually disappear

In Serenity Garden
The worldly sophistication is forgotten
The intellectuality of maturity is nurtured
The body is still in this world
The soul is already flying away

07/08/2016

50. 柔波里的水草

掩映着蓝天
生长在水底
柔波里的水草
婀娜着特有的风情

船桨划碎水底的天际
长篙撑出水波的涟漪
康河的柔波
荡出水草的柔情

昔人伤感的告别
赋予水草诗意的灵性
康河上下
引发痴迷者寻寻觅觅

静立水边
欣赏河里金柳的倒影
不经意间
邂逅了水草柔折的身形

一时默然无语
心头百感交集
水草依旧
欲做水草的昔人何去

50. *The Waterplants in the Waves*

Setting off the blue sky
And growing in the water
The waterplants dance gracefully
In the waves of the River Cam

The oars strike the sky in the water
Punting produces the ripples on the waves
The waterplants are so tender
In the mild waves of the river

The melancholy farewell of Xu Zhimo
Has endowed the waterplants with poetic spirit
Which leads many poetry lovers to look for it
Both upstream and downstream

Standing by the river quietly
I admire the reflection
Of the golden willows attentively
Unintentionally I see the waterplants
Dancing in the water elegantly

I fall into silence immediately
And a mixture of feelings swarm in me
The waterplants are still there
But where is Xu
Who wanted to be a waterplant

天空依旧高远
白云依然飘逸
康河的柔波
依旧拥吻着水草
流水潺潺
呼唤昔人的诗情

然而
昔人已去
作别了一切
空余康河畔
痴人叹惋的余音

2016-07-08，11:55

The sky is still high and far
The clouds are still graceful and free
The tender waves in the River Cam
Still embrace and kiss the waterplants
While the flowing water
Is calling for Xu's poetic beauty

However
The poet has passed away
Saying farewell to everything
At the bank of the river
There are only sighs and laments of me

07/08/2016

51. 午夜

午夜骤醒
无思无眠
唯有混沌的感觉

一切
寂然无声
或许
连空气也在酣眠

总希望诸事顺意
无奈总是旁生枝节

静夜中
漆黑一片
意欲忘却一切
思维却越发活跃
所有的纠结
——浮现眼前

2016-07-10, 18:10

51. At Midnight

Waking up at midnight
I cannot go to sleep again
Everything is in a mess
While I am in chaos

Silence dominates everything
Even the air is sleeping soundly
I always wish everything would go well
But the result is always the opposite

At midnight
I am surrounded by boundless darkness
Intending to forget everything
But my mind betrays me
So I sink into more and more active thinking

All entanglements
Appear in front of me
One scene after another scene

07/10/2016

52. 遗忘

我以为
如果要互相遗忘
我一定在你忘记我之前
先把你忘记
却发现
自己总是盲目地自信

时日过去
我在你心里
已经了然无迹
可我脑海里
总能浮现你的身影

人
总是这么没有逻辑
总是这么不可理喻

想起过去
似乎也没有多少温馨
自然也不会留下多少甜蜜
我本该先于你忘记
缘何总是把你记起

就这样
一边谴责自己
一边却希冀你的音信
失望之余
再次决定
把你尘封在记忆里

2016-07-14, 21:49

52. Forgetting

I always think
If we have to forget each other
I will forget you first
Before you can forget me
But I only find
I am too confident of myself

Time is still flying
In your heart
I no longer occupy a territory
But in my mind
You are still lingering

Human beings
Are always illogical
And act unreasonably

Recalling the past
Does not always involve
Sweetness and happiness
I should have forgotten you first
But somehow
You still remain in my mind

I blame myself on one hand
On the other
I am looking forward to your message
In disappointment
I again pluck up determination
To put you at the back of my mind

07/14/2016

53. 水边风景

落霞满天
夕阳西下
月儿
迫不及待
悬挂于云山之上

桨声阵阵
船儿归港
天鹅
一如既往
悠闲地在水面游荡

风轻云淡
柔波微漾
夜幕降临之际
一切悄然入画

2016-07-14，20:40

53. *Waterside View*

On the western sky
Rosy clouds float slowly
Setting against the setting sun
The moon comes out early
Hanging over the seeming cloud mountains

The oars are pulling
The boats are returning
The swans are swimming in the river
As leisurely and gracefully as usual

The clouds are pale
While the breeze is blowing
Then everything quietly
Makes a wonderful painting

07/14/2016

54. 想你，在夜半时分

夜半
寂静主宰一切
你的影像
穿越夜空
在我的眼睑边游荡

多想
与你漫步在草地
看素雅的野花
闻青草的馨香

多想
与你坐在剑河畔
听桨声哗然
观天鹅扑翅飞翔

多想
与你迤逦在树荫下
披着斑驳的树影
细数甜蜜的时光

梦里
我乘一叶扁舟
沿剑河漂流而下
独自体验行舟的浪漫
却有那成双的天鹅和野鸭
残忍地嘲笑我的孤单

2016-07-15, 07:50

54. *Missing You at Midnight*

At midnight
Silence dominates the universe
You quietly come through the space
And appear in front of my eyes

I wish
I could take a walk with you on the grass
Enjoying the elegant wild flowers
And smelling the grass' fragrance

I wish
I could sit with you
At the bank of the River Cam
Watching the oars rippling the water
And the swans flying over the river

I wish
I could stroll under the trees with you
Stepping on the tree shadows
And recalling the sweet memories

In the dream
I board a small boat
And go downstream on the River Cam
I experience the romance of punting
While the swans and wild ducks in pairs
Ruthlessly ridicule my solitude

07/15/2016

55. 自信

你是最好的
大家都同意
反对的
偏偏是你自己

为什么
总是这么没有自信
难道你不知道
自信是制胜的必备心理

只要不犯法
只要不害人
想做的事情
尽可以去尝试
成功了
是梦想的实现
失败了
是难得的经历

很多事情
重要的是过程
而不是结局
如此
对最后的结果
又何必那么在意

别人说你是最好的
那是一种鼓励
如果你自己也这么认为
这便是一种决心

55. Confidence

Everyone agrees
You are the best
The only one that disagrees
Is yourself

Why are you so diffident
Don't you know
Confidence is necessary
To succeed in everything

If you want to do something
Just do it
Unless it is illegal and harmful
If you succeed
You will realize your dream
If you fail
You will get special experience

For many doings
The process is more important
Than the final outcome
Therefore
Just ignore the ending
Even if it is misery

When others say you are the best
Regard it as encouragement
If you yourself think so
It is a kind of resolution

你是最好的
大家都同意
这其中
一定要包括你自己

2016-07-15，23:51

Everyone agrees
You are the best
And you yourself
Should also be included

07/15/2016

56. 薰衣草

逶迤林间小径
心怀寻美心情
高贵而典雅的薰衣草
吸引爱花之人远足而行

一片紫色的花海
开在天与地之间
高贵却并不冷漠
典雅却不失风情

一畦畦花垄
绵延至天际
犹如紫色的缎带
宛若通天路径

天路尽头
蓝天高远
白云飘荡
毫无疑问
花海的那一边
便是人们向往的天堂

逶迤在花垄间
没入花海深处
视线所及
是花的绰约风姿
沁入心脾
是花独特的香气
侧耳倾听
则是花蕊的唱吟

56. *Lavender*

With the wish of looking for beauty
I stroll on the trail in the forest
The noble and elegant lavender
Induces me to take an outskirt trip

Between the sky and the earth
Blooms a purple sea of flowers
Noble and passionate
With elegance and romance

The flowerbeds stretch out to the skyline
Just like purple satin ribbons
Leading a way to a mysterious place

At the far end lies the blue sky
With the white clouds floating high
Undoubtedly
Beyond the flower sea
Lies the paradise
Longed for by the human being

Walking among the flowerbeds
I hide myself in the flower sea
I am surrounded by the elegance
And intoxicated with the fragrance
The singing of the flower hearts
Enriches me with sweetness

喜欢是一种权利
爱慕是一种自由
喜欢和爱慕
无须别人准许
亦不需要理由
一如我对薰衣草的爱
不是矫情的造作
而是心灵深处的倾心

采一把薰衣草
把美带回家
枕着花香入眠
薰衣草
成了我梦中所念

2016-07-18，19:11

To like is a right
To love is freedom
In terms of love or adoration
You need neither reason nor permission
Just like my love to lavender
It is not hypocritical pretension
But a call from the bottom of my heart

I pick up a bunch of lavender
And bring it back home
I sleep with the fragrance
And in the dream
Lavender becomes my company

07/18/2016

57. 心桥

这里暗
那里明
这里夜色迷离
那里太阳升起

这里
水波涌动
激起无限的柔情
那里
人流如潮
淹没忙碌的身影

月色寄托的相思
被忙碌所背弃
这里的思念愈浓
那里的回应愈稀
思念最终流落天际
遗落一地无奈的叹息

忙碌你身
失落我心
希冀有一双万能的手
搭建一座无形的心桥
让我走进你的心里

2016-7-21，18:16

57. The Heart Bridge

Here where I live
It is nighttime
There where you live
It is daytime
Here
Night resumes her reign
There
The sun is rising

Here
The waves are swarming
Rippling with limitless tenderness
There
People are everywhere
Submerging your busy body

The yearning for you in the moonlight
Is betrayed by being busy
The more I miss you
The less response I get
The yearning then goes to exile
Leaving helpless sighs everywhere

You are busy
And frustration overwhelms me
I wish
A pair of omnipotent hands
Would build a bridge
To lead me into your heart

07/21/2016

58. 聚散两依依

离你很远的时候
心却靠得很近
离你很近的时候
心却理性偏离

有些感觉
只是瞬息间的会意
一个眼神
传递某种爱意
一个动作
显露些许柔情

话语汩汩
无须刻意
当不得不说再见
居然有了不舍的离情

相聚是过程
分离是结局
喜相聚
伤别离
聚散两依依

独坐河畔
任清风拂面
纾解孤寂
却有那忙碌的蜂儿
暗自讪笑人的痴情

2016-07-23, 07:29

58. Reluctant Meeting and Parting

When far away from you
I feel close to you in heart
When close to you
My heart sensibly
Wanders away from you

Some certain perception
Is only momentary understanding
A glance
Is to deliver deep love
An action
Is to manifest tender feeling

Talks between you and me
Are not painstaking
When we have to part
Both feel reluctant to do it

Meeting is the process
While parting is the ending
Happy to meet
Melancholy to part
Either situation makes us feel reluctant

Sitting at the riverside
I ease my solitude with the wind blowing
But the busy bees
Are ridiculing my vain love secretly

07/23/2016

59. 圣保罗大教堂的钟声

夜晚
钟声送我入眠
清晨
钟声把我催醒

悠扬的钟声
不变的旋律
历史
不管人间悲情
不紧不慢地前行

钟声响起
梦境依稀
混沌中
挫败感压倒一切
淹没业已动摇的自信

圣人
之所以为圣
是因为坚定不移
一如那钟声
不管人们接受与否
千古不变
萦绕在耳际
俨然一种警醒

剖析自己
昭示心灵
默默地礼拜
自己心中确立的上帝

2016-08-07, 08:07

59. The Bell Ring of St. Paul's Cathedral

At night
The rings of the bell lull me to sleep
At daybreak
The rings of the bell wake me up

The bell goes on to ring
With consistent melody
While history
Paying no attention to human sorrow
Goes forward with changeless paces

When the bell rings aloud
The dream is still clear in mind
In chaotic mood
Frustration is overwhelming
Which defeats the uncertain confidence

The saints become saintly
Because of their belief and persistence
Just like the ringing of the bell
No matter whether people accept it or not
It rings regularly
Haunting the ears of human beings
As a kind of warning

To reveal my own soul
By way of analyzing
I silently pray to the God
Established by myself in my heart

08/07/2016

60. 心乱

孤寂
自心底而起
如教堂的尖顶
孑然
傲然
决然
直达天际

走过很多神的居所
还是无法走近上帝
慰藉的心音
无处可寻

大脑释放的信息
杂乱无序
心也乱了
焦虑不已
耳际鸣响绞心的噪音

是因为时日的逝去
还是因为不舍的离情
很多事情
无法抗拒
无谓的挣扎
只能破坏宁静的心情

说服自己
学会放弃
让心宁静
及至远方
寻觅久违的诗意

2016-08-11, 10:18

60. *Messy Mood*

Like the spire of the cathedral
Solitude rises from inside
Lonely
Proud
Determined
It then drifts faraway to the sky

Having visited many God's habitations
I still cannot get close to Him
The voice of consolation
Is far away from me

Messages let out by the brain
Are completely disorderly
The mood is messy
The heart is filled with noise of anxiety

Is it because time is flying
Or I feel reluctant to leave
Many things cannot be prevented
Useless struggles
Can only lead to uneasiness

Persuade myself to give up
Let the heart
Travel to the remote places
Looking for the long-forgotten poetry

08/11/2016

61. 时间很长，爱情很短

时间很长
爱情很短
在时光隧道的某一点
驻足回望
爱
已经烟消云散

穿越时空的守候
最终守成了失望
遗落的承诺
随风飘散
化成缥缈的流沙

流沙吞噬了绿洲
蚕食仅有的心念
爱情之树
不再生长

时间很长
爱情很短
看沙漏不断
叹情感无常
无谓的爱
沉落时间长河
成为河底的泥沙

2016-08-11, 10:35

61. *Time and Love*

Time is long
Love is transient
At a certain moment in the time tunnel
You stop and look back
Only to find
Love has already disappeared

The waiting through time and space
Turns out to be disappointment in the end
The deserted promise
Has been driven away
Becoming the misty drifting sand

The drifting sand destroys the oases
And nips away the only concern
The tree of love
Stops to grow up

Time is long
Love is transient
The hourglass never stops running
Feeling never stops changing
Meaningless love
Sinks into the river of time
And becomes sand at the bottom

08/11/2016

62. 月季花咏

不需邂逅
已有太多的相遇
在邻居的院落中
在皇家的花园里

为了展示美丽
延长了一季的花期
风过处
绰约摇曳出花香
细雨中
雨丝飘落出神韵

缤纷的色彩
装点的何止是季节
还有爱花的心情

花儿美丽
岁月如此静好
就算悠悠流逝
亦不辜负流年
绝无悔意

清风拂面
花儿颔首
对惜花人点头致意

2016-08-13，20:35

62. *Ode to Chinese Roses*

We don't meet unexpectedly
We have met many many times
In the front yards of the neighbors
And in the royal gardens

In order to display your beauty
You prolong the season of blossoming
You emit your fragrance in the wind
And show your charm in the rain

The variety of colors
Not only modifies the season
But also pleases the heart of flower lovers

The flowers are so beautiful
And the days are so quiet
Though time is flying
It is worthy of living
With no regrets and irritancy

When the wind rises again
The flowers are nodding gracefully
To greet the flower lovers gaily

08/13/2016

63. 结局

落霞满天
如血
心如止水
静卧宁静的水面

天鹅
若无其事地夜游
牛不知归
把草地当成了家园

残存的牵挂
不再寄托中天的月
承诺如昨
却成了善意的谎言

偶尔想起
宛如昨日再现
心动依旧
却已不再心痛
曾经的感动
思之却已久远

晚霞落幕之时
愿你我安然入眠
无梦
无忧
无怨

2016-08-13，21:24

63. *The Ending*

The rosy evening clouds are red as blood
My mind remains calm
Just like the still water

The swans are swimming in the river
As if nothing were in their mind
The cattle stay on the grassland
Regarding it as their pen

The surviving concern
Does not rely on the expression of the moon
The promise is still around the ears
Yet it has become a white lie

Occasionally
The past comes back to me clearly
I am still moved
But not sorrowful at all
And the touching affection
Seems to be lifetime away

When the rosy evening clouds disappear
I wish
Both of us could go to sleep soundly
Without dreams
Without depression
Without complaints

08/13/2016

64. 心情即景

天光云影
金柳依依
曾经的憧憬
随夕阳西下
在西天边上流浪

希望
总在海的那一边
失落的种子
无须雨露的滋润
破土发芽
开出令人心痛的花

牛群
纵然迟归
也有自己的巢厩
缘何
凌乱的心
总是找不到归宿

剑河的水
依旧宁静
致远的心境
却无处可寻

天光已暗
牛群不归
繁杂的思绪
依旧飘飞如烟雨
于是
心情的天空
下起了绵绵细雨

2016-08-16，20:22

64. *Mood and Landscape*

The clouds are floating in the sky
The golden willows are swaying on the land
The once-cherished longing
Is hanging around in the western sky
And will perish with the fading sunlight

Hope
Lies on the other coast of the sea
The seed of despair
Even if without watering
Sprouts out of the soil
And blooms against the heart's desire

The cattle will go back late
But they have their own pen
While my chaotic heart
Is always roaming about
Finding no harbor to stay

Water in the River Cam
Is as peaceful as ever
But peacefulness in mind
Is nowhere to find

It is getting dark
But the cattle are still on the grassland
Irritancy lingers in mind
Like misty rain
Which results in drizzling
In the sky of moody mind

08/16/2016

65. 莫名

莫名的忧烦
在心里
依旧起居如常
一样欢声笑语
心绪
却总不得安宁

此时
看天鹅不再悠闲
看牛群不再适意
连天上的白云
也已不再飘逸

却有那只孤鸟
伫立枝头独鸣
莫哀
莫哀
归期已经临近

2016-08-17，11:51

65. *Inexplicable Mood*

Inexplicable frets
Dwell in my heart
Though I live as usual
With cheerful chatting and laughing
My mind cannot enjoy peace

Under this circumstance
The swans seem not leisurely
The cattle seem not happy
Even the clouds in the sky
Seem not graceful and free

Only the lonely bird
Is perching on the twig
Singing the sympathetic notes
Don't worry
Don't worry
The day of homecoming is approaching

08/17/2016

66. 焦虑

一种无奈
袭上心头
焦虑
总在梦魇之后

云儿收起了翅膀
柳枝总在垂泪
鸟儿已经噤声
花儿行将枯萎

天气依然晴好
心情郁闷如昔
整个世界
成了炼狱
灼伤焦虑的心

太阳照样升起
心绪繁杂无序
茫然无措
仰天问询
何处去寻
救赎我的上帝

2016-08-17，09:39

66. *Anxiety*

A feeling of impotence
Overwhelms me
Frets come always after nightmares

The clouds are not floating
The golden willows are always weeping
The birds stop singing
The flowers are about to lose their beauty

The weather is still fine
But the mood is blue
The whole world becomes purgatory
And the worrying heart is scorching

The sun also rises
While the frets still haunt me
In despair
I raise my head to the sky
And ask God
Where I can find my savior

08/17/2017

67. 平衡

很多时候
需要安静
因为喧嚣过于沉重
人的心脏
负荷不起

有的时候
需要声音
因为沉静太过彻底
威胁业已脆弱的神经

任何时候
需要内心的定力
若否
心将碎裂
内心成为一片废墟

总是说服自己
该放弃的就要放弃
让喧嚣和沉静
趋于平衡
让自己的内心
趋于平静

无论如何
让眼睛看到美好
让内心感受温情
让世界成为风景

2016-08-19，17:03

67. Balance

Most of the time
People need quietness
As human hearts
Cannot stand the annoying noise

However
We need voice sometimes
As the utmost silence
Will threaten the weak nerves

Anytime
Consistent inward ability is needed
Otherwise
The heart will split
And the mind will be in ruin

I always persuade myself
To give up when necessary
So as to keep a balance
Between noise and silence
Let the heart tend to be peaceful

Anyway
I should try my best
To see nice things with my eyes
To feel the tenderness with my heart
To help the world become landscapes

08/19/2016

68. 迫不及待的秋天

在夏天的葱绿中
看到秋天的影
迫不及待的秋天
正在驱赶洋洋得意的夏季

无情
在驱赶中成立
纵使秋天美丽
喧宾夺主的无理
折损了秋天的魅力

凝视秋天的影
看到了秋季的自己
华发已生
余年无几
时间
还在不紧不慢地前行

虽然伤感
但不悲戚
随心顺意
想坚持便坚持
该放弃便放弃
直至进入永久的栖息地

2016-08-19，17:30

68. Impatient Autumn

In summer's green
I see the trace of autumn
It is so eager to come on stage
That it tries to drive away the arrogant summer

In so doing
Ruthlessness comes into being
Though autumn is beautiful
It reduces its charm
By intruding on summer rudely

Gazing at the autumn's trace
I see myself in the autumn of life
Hair has turned grey
The life journey is shorter and shorter
But time
Is still advancing mercilessly

Though I feel a little bit sad
But not so discouraged
I will follow my heart's desires
To persist if I want
To give up if necessary
Until the permanent resting place
Is in front of me

08/19/2016

69. 剑桥天气即景

蓝天白云
晴空万里
忽然
一片乌云来袭
太阳
退出了已经占领的领地

风起雨密
屋檐滴雨
路人加快步子
躲进自己的蜗居

瞬息万变的天气
一如无着的心情
有时灿烂如阳光
有时阴郁如骤雨

天地间
多了一个
哀愁上瘾的生灵

2016-08-19，17:46

69. *The Weather in Cambridge*

The sunlit sky is blue and clear
With white clouds floating near
Suddenly
A black cloud comes over
Forcing the sun to disappear

The wind rises and the rain pours down
Rainwater drips from the eves
The passersby quicken their paces
To hurry back to their houses

The fast changing weather
Is just like the lonesome mood
Sometimes it is shining
Sometimes it is rainy

Between the sky and the land
There exists a living creature
Who indulges herself in solitude

08/19/2016

70. 无言的陪伴

独立枝头
你是慰藉灵魂的使者
初达英伦
你行欢迎之礼
慰问我于清冷的晨曦

在我孤寂之际
你在枝头独鸣
或许
你在吟唱自己的心情
于我
则是驱除孤独的旋律

再访英伦
你是第一个造访的生灵
见到你
犹如老友重逢
一切不如意
尽皆遁迹

你是否也知道
我的归期已近
你的到来
是否是告别之举

当我携梦归去
你无言的陪伴
从此进入我的梦里

2016-08-19, 18:19

70. Silent Company

Perching on the twig alone
You are the massager of consolation to my soul
When I first arrived in England
You welcomed me in the early morning
Giving me comforting greetings

When I felt lonely
You were singing on the tree
Maybe you were chanting
About your own feeling
To me
It was melody to drive away anxiety

The second time I came to England
You were the first one to visit me
You were somewhat like my old friend
At the sight of you
Unhappiness just refrained from me

Do you also know
Farewell is coming
So you again come to see me
Also to say goodbye to me

When I leave with my dreams
Your silent company
Will no doubt go into my sleep

08/19/2016

71. 我想，我是把你弄丢了

此时此刻
在剑河边
我们应该一起
看天鹅戏水
观落日余晖
我想
我是把你弄丢了
剩下我一人
形只影单

景色很美
美得令人心醉
我们应该一起
观波光潋滟
听潺潺流水
我想
我是把你弄丢了
景色虽美
却看不到你的影像

河边的步道
宁静而悠长
我们应该一起
漫步步道
闲话人生
你嗔怪我的散漫
我嗤笑你的狂妄
我想
我是把你弄丢了
听你的声音
成了无法实现的梦想

71. I Must Have Lost You

At this very moment
We should be together at the River Cam
Looking at the swans swimming
And the sun setting
I think
I must have lost you
So that I am right here by myself
All alone

The scenery is very beautiful
Intoxicating and fascinating
We should be together
Looking at the ripples on the river
And listening to the murmur
Of the flowing water
I think
I must have lost you
So that you are not here with me
And enjoy the beautiful scenery

The footpath at the riverbank
Is quiet and long
We should be together
Taking walks along the river
And talking about life
Maybe you would blame me
For my sloppiness
And I would laugh at your ambitions
I think
I must have lost you
So that it is only illusion
To hear your voice

夕阳
照样西下
金柳
还是夕阳中的新娘
可我想
我是把你弄丢了
夜色向晚
望断天涯
也不知你在何方

一路走来
是我把你遗落在路上
抑或是你偏离了方向
我想
我是把你弄丢了
也许
正应验了那句话
走着走着
不知不觉
就散了

2016-08-20，21:17

The sun is setting down
And the golden willow
Is still the bride of the setting sun
I think I must have lost you
So that I do not know where your are
When it is getting dark

All the way along
Is it that I have lost you somewhere
Or you yourself deviate from the direction
I think
I must have lost you
Maybe the saying is absolutely true
That we used to walk together harmoniously
But as time goes on
We just wander off

08/20/2016

72. 月夜怀想

黄昏
静坐水边
目送夕阳西下
不经意间回眸
天边
挂着一轮月亮

也想
披着如洗的月光
与你漫步在苍穹下
听夜虫的低吟
沐夜色的柔光
谈文学的魅力
论情感的短长

也想
依着你的伟岸
在草地上徜徉
或则躺在杂草中
借月亮的微光
看你坚毅的面庞

也想
听你狂妄的言谈
抑或是奇怪的梦想
在月夜的孤岛上
作为岛主
用小提琴拉出奇幻的乐章

72. Thinking at Moon Night

At dusk
I sit at the waterside
Saying goodbye to the sun
I unintentionally look back
On the other side of the sky
And find the moon is already there

I wish
I could take a walk with you
Under the sky in the moonlight
Listening to the insects' singing
And enjoying the tender night
We would also
Talk about the charm of literature
And the right and wrong of love

I wish
I could get close to your strong body
And stroll with you on the grassland
Or lie on the grass
Looking at your determined face
In the tender moonlight

I wish
I could listen to your ambitious talks
Or your peculiar dream
In it
As the master of the lonely island
You are completely engrossed in
Playing amazing melodies with violin

月凉如水
甜蜜的憧憬
挡不住月夜的微寒
千里之外
是否也有一个魂灵
同样在仰视清冷的月亮

2016-08-20，19:14

The moonlight is as cool as water
The sweet yearnings
Cannot fight back the slight chilliness
I am not sure
Whether there is a soul
Who is also looking at the chilly moon
On the other half of the earth

08/20/2016

73. 不止一辈子

已经过去了多少年月
我总在尽力长大
如今
我俨然已经高大挺拔
而我的一辈子
已经比很多生灵更长

我已经鼓足勇气
坦然面对死亡
然而
我不会彻底烟消云散
我的生命
已经重生在别的地方

你看
树干下美丽的花
还有正在酿蜜的蜂儿
它们身上
都有我生命的影像

我的一辈子
并不短暂
不同生命的汇入
使之更加
恒久
绵长

2016-08-26, 23:03

73. More than One Life

For many years
I have tried my best to grow up
Now I am already tall and big
And I have lived longer
Than many living things

I am brave enough
To confront death
However
I will not disappear
As I have transferred my life
Into other lives

See the beautiful flowers beneath my body
And the bees are making them into honey
So my life flows into many lives

My life is not short
With many other lives in my body
I can live more than one life

08/26/2016

74. 那一晚

那一晚
夜色凄厉
本就不适合心的旅行
你却执意要与我同行
最终
你我迷失在荒郊野地

那一晚
月色惨白
白得令人痛心
我想
我一定是面如死灰
让你绝望到了心底

于是
你宁愿睡去
不愿再听我的呓语
我愕然
你的承诺
竟然如此不堪一击

浪漫的期许
无语的结局

意念里
早已抹去那一晚的记忆
让夜的黑
隐去爱的杂音

74. On That Night

On that night
It was forlorn and bitter
So that it was not suitable
For the souls to travel
Yet we did it
Then both of us
Lost ourselves in wilderness

On that night
The moonlight was so gloomy
That it made us so moody
I think
My face must have been deadly pale
And you were completely in despair

Therefore
You'd rather go to sleep
Instead of listening to my crazy talks
I was so startled
That your promise was as fragile as glass

Romantic expectation at the beginning
Unfruitful ending in the end

In my mind
I have already erased the memory
On that night
I also let the darkness of the night
Conceal the cacophonous love music

那一晚
出发时有你相伴
归程时踽踽独行
仰头望月
月亮惨白依旧
为无缘的你我
轻轻叹息

2016-08-28，0:25

On that night
I began the trip with your company
But came back all alone by myself
I looked up at the moon
It was as pale as before
Sighing on the bad luck
Both for you and for me

08/28/2016

75. 离歌

清秋渐近
离情已浓
太多的不舍
遗落无奈的匆匆

金柳垂泪
剑河不语
离情别绪
弥漫到傲然的天际

空中的云絮
是否不舍的呓语
婀娜的水草
是否摇曳出悲戚

秋近了
月凉了
玲珑的秋月
笼罩着离人
唱响心底的离歌

2016-09-01，20:04

75. The Song of Leaving

The clear autumn is coming
The day of leaving is approaching
Though I feel much reluctant to leave
Time is still flying

The golden willows are weeping
While the River Cam keeps silent
Sorrow and feeling of leaving
Spread into the arrogant sky

The clouds are expressing
The wistful ravings
The graceful waterplants
Are swaying with sadness

Autumn is coming
The moonlight is chilly
The charming and beautiful moon
Shines on me
Who is singing the song of leaving

09/01/2016

76. 离情

纵有千般不舍
终究还须离别
离情
化成天上的云絮
飘忽不定
搅扰惯有的心静

别了
河畔的金柳
别了
剑河的涟漪
别了
醉人的美景
别了
剑桥特有的诗意

千般愁
万缕情
友情
柔情
诗情
一切
一切的一切
从此魂牵梦萦

2016-09-01，18:40

76. *Feeling of Leaving*

Though I feel much reluctant
I have to leave finally
The feeling of leaving
Transforms into clouds in the sky
Floating aimlessly
And disturbing the everlasting peacefulness

Goodbye
The golden willows at the riverbank
Goodbye
The ripples on the River Cam
Goodbye
Intoxicating sceneries
Goodbye
Poetic and romantic Cambridge

Sadness and tenderness
Love and friendship
Poetry and everything
I will keep all of them
In my memory

09/01/2016